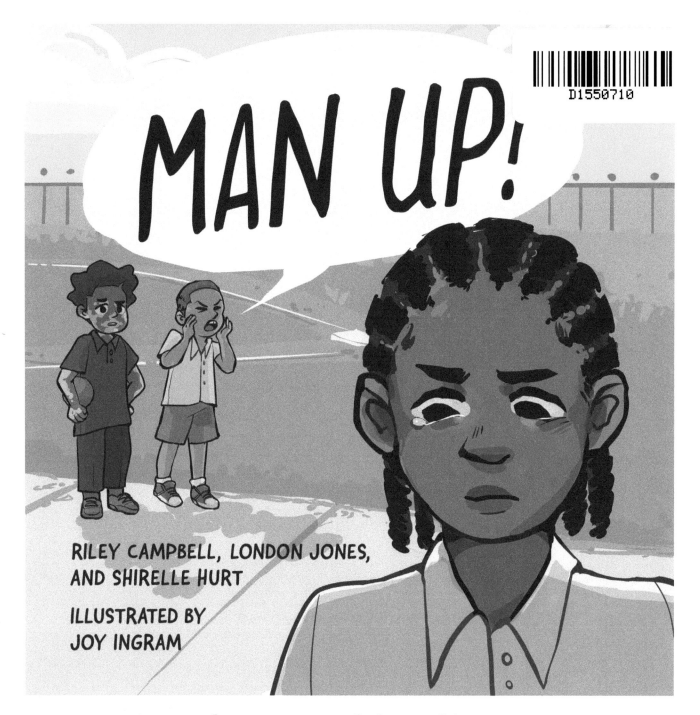

MAN UP!

RILEY CAMPBELL, LONDON JONES,
AND SHIRELLE HURT

ILLUSTRATED BY
JOY INGRAM

Reach Incorporated | Washington, DC

Shout Mouse Press

Reach Education, Inc. / Shout Mouse Press
Published by
Shout Mouse Press, Inc.

Shout Mouse Press is a nonprofit writing and publishing program dedicated to amplifying underheard voices. This book was produced through Shout Mouse workshops and in collaboration with Shout Mouse artists and editors.

Shout Mouse coaches writers from marginalized communities to tell their own stories in their own voices and, as published authors, to act as agents of change. In partnership with other nonprofit organizations serving communities in need, we are building a catalog of inclusive, mission-driven books that engage reluctant readers as well as open hearts and minds.

Learn more and see our full catalog at www.shoutmousepress.org.

For all the boys who are told
they can't be themselves.

It's the weekend!

Aaron and his friends are so excited. There's so much to do! They want to have a Forknife tournament, play kickball, and eat five HUNDRED oatmeal cream pies.

Aaron can't wait. He loves chilling with his friends.
There's only one problem.
Everybody calls Aaron a crybaby.

That night, Aaron and his crew are playing a video game tournament. Aaron really wants to win a new Forknife skin. But his friends cheat, and Aaron gets angry.

"Ay bruh, I know you used a code!"

He tries to call out his friends, but they just laugh at him.

He feels powerless and starts to cry.

"Get over it!"

"Don't be such a wuss!"

"You're acting like a girl."

"Tighten up, it's just a game!"

"You're such a punk."

Aaron wipes his tears and challenges his friends to a rematch.

The next day, Aaron and his friends are playing kickball at Deanwood Rec.

Aaron is in left field, telling jokes.

"Hey Derrick," Aaron yells, "how does the ocean say hi? It WAVES!!"

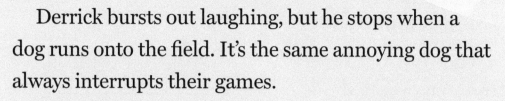

Derrick bursts out laughing, but he stops when a dog runs onto the field. It's the same annoying dog that always interrupts their games.

"Hey dirty mutt, get out the way!" Derrick yells.

"Mooooove!" says Aaron.

Derrick starts chasing the dog, and Tayshawn picks up a rock and throws it.

The rock hits the dog!

The dog yelps, and Tayshawn and Derrick start laughing.

Aaron runs over to the dog to see if she's OK. She limps away.

"She's hurt! Why would you do that?" Aaron looks like he's about to cry.

"Look at the cryyybaby," Tayshawn says with a grin.

Tears stream down Aaron's face and he runs off the field.

When Aaron gets home, he tries to FaceTime his older brother, Sage.

But Sage texts him and says, "I can't talk right now. I have a midterm on Monday."

Aaron sighs and covers his face with a pillow. He feels alone. He wishes he had someone to talk to.

Aaron hears his father calling him for dinner. He doesn't answer. Quickly, he wipes the tears off his face with his shirt. He can't let his dad see him upset.

But when Aaron opens the door to go wash his hands, he is startled to find his father right outside his room.

"What's wrong with your eyes?" his dad asks.

"Nothing." Aaron looks at the floor.

"I know you were crying. What's going on?"

Aaron tells his dad about the video game and the dog and Sage not answering his call.

His dad just shakes his head.

"Maybe your friends are right. Maybe you need to stop crying so much. You need to man up! Leave that crying for the girls."

On Monday, Aaron sits alone on the school bus, feeling sad.

Blair, his neighbor, walks by. Aaron notices a doll dangling from her hand.

"Your doll is pretty," Aaron says, trying to cheer himself up.

"Ew, you like dolls?!" Blair frowns and says, "Dolls are for girls!"

Darius, the nosy kid, overhears.

He stands up and yells, "Guess what, everybody? Aaron likes dolls!"

The whole bus starts laughing and chanting, "AARON LIKES DOLLS."

Aaron feels overwhelmed.
He thinks about what his
dad told him, to man up.
He stands and squares up,
looking straight at Darius.

But suddenly the bus jerks and he falls back into his seat.

Ooooof!

Everybody laughs again.

Aaron just turns around and puts his earphones in. He doesn't want to fight anyway. He knows how it feels to get hurt. Instead, he cries.

When Aaron gets home, Sage is there waiting for him... with roller skates!

His dad says, "Look who's here. He came to surprise you."

Sage says, "Hey man, sorry for ghosting you. Wanna go to Crystal's?"

Aaron feels better right away.

While they are skating, Sage asks Aaron, "So why did you call me the other day?"

Aaron takes a deep breath. "Sage, do you cry?" he asks.

"Sometimes, when I feel overwhelmed. Is that why you called me? To talk about crying?"

"Everyone calls me a crybaby. It makes me feel like I should run away. I know I should man up, but... "

Aaron looks away from his brother, embarrassed.

"Let's get some pizza and talk about it," Sage says.

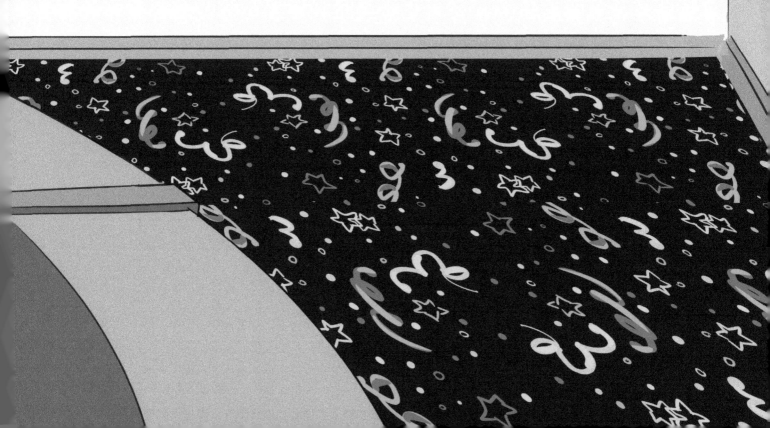

When they sit down, Sage says,

"Look, little bro. It's OK to cry. It took me years to learn that, though. Dad taught me that crying is for girls, but after I went to college, I realized that crying is normal."

"Normal? Nobody acts like it's normal. Not for boys at least."

"Well they're wrong. It releases stress, which is something I need sometimes. If you keep it pent up inside, you get angry. And too much anger is not good for anybody."

Aaron is confused. "Stop playing. So why is everyone telling me crying is bad?"

"That's just what they've been taught. They don't know how to handle their emotions. But we can try to end this. How about I'll talk to Dad and you can handle them other little rascals."

Aaron starts laughing. "Rascals? What are you, like 60?"

The next day, Aaron, Derrick, and Tayshawn are all chilling at Deanwood Rec with Sage. Tayshawn starts to make fun of Aaron again, but Aaron cuts him off.

"Get off my back! You know what? Crying is actually good for you."

Tayshawn and Derrick both laugh like hyenas.

Aaron's eyes start to water, but Sage speaks up for him.

"Y'all never get sad? What about when your parents fight, or somebody lets you down? It's OK to get sad. Crying lets your friends know you need support."

Tayshawn and Derrick look at him funny.

"Saying 'don't cry' is like saying 'don't ever tell anyone you're sad.' That's not healthy."

Sage gets up. "Y'all need to work this out." He nods at Aaron and walks away.

Tayshawn rolls his eyes.

"Sorry, bruh. Your brother's cool, but nah, you're just being a crybaby," Tayshawn says.

"I don't know, I think maybe we've been too mean," Derrick says.

"No, I'm trying to help him. Aaron needs to man up."

"Why?" says Aaron. "Didn't you just hear how that's bad for you?"

"But that's what we do! That's how life is!"

Tayshawn pushes Aaron and runs away.

"You OK, man?" Derrick asks.

"Yeah," says Aaron. "Thanks for sticking up for me."

"You know how Tayshawn is."

"Yeah, we should go check on him."

When they find him, Tayshawn is kicking rocks and dirt. He's holding back tears.

"What's wrong?" Derrick asks.

"Nothing!" Tayshawn screams.

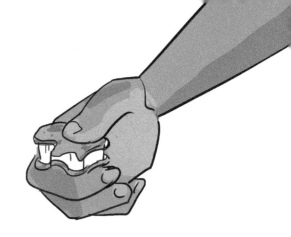

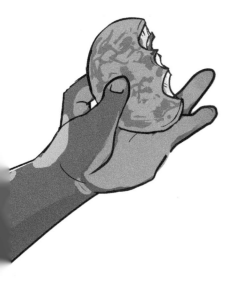

Aaron pulls out three cream pies from his backpack and hands one to Tayshawn.

"This is how you're going to cheer me up?" Tayshawn laughs.

"Bruh, I'm sorry if I hurt your feelings. Even if you were being a baby," says Tayshawn.

"Not cool, man," Derrick says.

"What? He's got it easy. I mean, he has Sage. I don't have no one to talk to," says Tayshawn.

"You could talk to me," Aaron says.

Tayshawn shakes his head.

"You gonna still help me after I was mean?"

"If you promise to stop calling me a crybaby."

Tayshawn laughs. "That's a bet."

About the Authors

Riley Campbell
is a sixteen-year-old junior at Ballou Senior High School. She likes to do artistic things, travel, and listen to music. She wrote this book because toxic masculinity is a topic that isn't talked about, but is a major problem in our society. She hopes readers understand that gender is a social construct — you can be whoever you want to be.

London Jones
is a fifteen-year-old sophomore at Anacostia High School. He likes to sit at home, mind his business, stay in his place, and put you in yours. He loves watching TV and his dream job is to be a famous journalist. This is his first book. He wants readers to get that there's no such thing as "girly" or "boyish" emotions. Be yourself no matter what.

Shirelle Hurt
is a seventeen-year-old junior at Dunbar High School. She likes to explore and go places like museums and the National Harbor. She also likes to watch Netflix and eat snacks. She hopes readers will understand that it's OK for boys to show their emotions.

Barrett Smith served as Story Coach for this book.

Hayes Davis served as Head Story Coach for this year's series.

About the Illustrator

Joy Ingram

is a student in Communication Arts at Virginia Commonwealth University in Richmond. She is interested in portraying stories through art and showcasing under-represented communities. She loves using bright colors and finds inspiration from her Caribbean American background. She is interested in digital artwork and children's illustration. You can view more of her work at joyingram.portfoliobox.net.

Writers and artists at work

Acknowledgments

For the seventh summer in a row, teens from Reach Incorporated were issued a challenge: compose original children's books that will both educate and entertain young readers. Specifically, these teens were asked to create inclusive stories that reflect their lived experiences, so that every child has the opportunity to relate to characters on the page. And for the seventh summer in a row, these teens have demonstrated that they know their audience, they believe in their mission, and they take pride in the impact they can make on young lives.

Thirteen writers spent the month of July brainstorming ideas, generating potential plots, writing, revising, and providing critiques. Authoring quality books is challenging work, and these authors have our immense gratitude and respect: Jesse, Jailah, Victoria, Jocktavious, Talik, Anaya, Dewan, Riley, London, Shirelle, Camal, Japan, and Dameona.

These books represent an ongoing collaboration between Reach Incorporated and Shout Mouse Press, and we are grateful for the leadership provided by members of both teams. From Reach, Anika Rich contributed meaningfully to discussions and morale, and the Reach summer program leadership of Kim Davis and Jusna Perrin kept us organized and well-equipped. From the Shout Mouse Press team, we thank Head Story Coach Hayes Davis, who oversaw this year's workshops, and Story Coaches Barrett Smith, Marisa Kwaning, Faith Campbell, and Amy Sawyer for bringing both fun and insight to the project. We can't thank enough illustrators Camryn Simms, Anthony White, Joy Ingram, and India Valle for bringing these stories to life with their beautiful artwork. Finally, Amber Colleran brought a keen eye and important mentorship to the project as the series Art Director and book designer. We are grateful for the time and talents of these writers and artists!

Finally, we thank those of you who have purchased books and cheered on our authors. It is your support that makes it possible for these teen authors to engage and inspire young readers. We hope you smile as much while you read as these teens did while they wrote.

Mark Hecker   Kathy Crutcher
Reach Incorporated   Shout Mouse Press

About Reach Incorporated  Reach

Reach Incorporated develops readers and leaders by preparing teens to serve as tutors and role models for younger students, resulting in improved literacy outcomes for the teen tutors and their elementary school students.

Founded in 2009, Reach recruits high school students to be elementary school reading tutors. After completing a year in our program, teens gain access to additional leadership development opportunities, including The Summer Leadership Academy, The College Mentorship Program, and The Reach Fellowship. Through this comprehensive system of supports, teens are prepared to thrive in high school and beyond.

Through their work as reading tutors, our teens noticed that the books they read with their students did not always reflect their lived experiences. As always, we felt the best way we could address this issue was to put our teens in charge. Through our collaboration with Shout Mouse Press, these teens create engaging stories with diverse characters that invite young readers to explore the world through words.

By purchasing our books, you support student-led, community-driven efforts to improve educational outcomes in the District of Columbia.

Learn more at www.reachincorporated.org.

FEB 2 4 2020

CPSIA information can be obtained
at www.ICGtesting.com
Printed in the USA
LVHW071454200120
644156LV00022B/1831

9 781950 807055